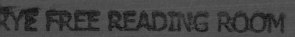

Hocus Pocus It's Fall!

BY Anne Sibley O'Brien

ILLUSTRATED BY Susan Gal

Abrams Appleseed
New York

Summer days
begin to cool.
Alakazam!

Spiky pods
are brown and dried.

Open sesame!

Geese and ducks
prepare to fly.
Zip and zing!

Leaves on trees
are green and bright.
Abracadabra!

Chilly gusts
toss leaves around.
Shazam!

Busy squirrels
fill their cheeks.
Abba zabba!

Bins of fruit are piled high.
Higgledy piggledy!

Pick a pumpkin,
orange and fat.

Razzle dazzle!

Chipmunks dig
their burrows deep.
Sim sala bim!

Put on a hat,
a woolly sweater.
Presto chango!

Wrap up tight
with winter near.

Hocus pocus!

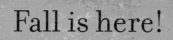

Fall is here!

For Taemin, all year round.
—ASO

For the nurses on 5 West, Sharp Memorial Hospital,
San Diego. All of you are forever in our hearts.
—SG

The illustrations in this book were made with
charcoal on paper and digital collage.

Cataloging-in-Publication Data has been applied for and
may be obtained from the Library of Congress.

ISBN: 978-1-4197-2125-0

Printed and bound in China
10 9 8 7 6 5 4 3 2

For bulk discount inquiries, contact specialsales@abramsbooks.com.

ABRAMS The Art of Books
115 West 18th Street, New York, NY 10011
abramsbooks.com